W9-DAG-725

12/2015

Level 1

THIS IS FALCON

Written by *Clarissa Wong*

Illustrated by *Ron Lim* and *Rachelle Rosenberg*

Based on the Marvel comic book series *The Avengers*

ABDO
Spotlight

MARVEL

Los Angeles
New York

ABDOPUBLISHING.COM

Reinforced library bound edition published in 2016 by Spotlight, a division of ABDO
PO Box 398166, Minneapolis, Minnesota 55439. Spotlight produces high-quality
reinforced library bound editions for schools and libraries. Published by Marvel Press,
an imprint of Disney Book Group.

Printed in the United States of America, North Mankato, Minnesota.
042015
092015

marvelkids.com
© 2015 MARVEL

LIBRARY OF CONGRESS CATALOGING-IN-PUBLICATION DATA

This title was previously cataloged with the following information:

Wong, Clarissa.
 Falcon : This is Falcon / written by Clarissa Wong ; illustrated by Ron Lim and Rachelle
Rosenberg.
  p. cm. (World of reading ; Level 1)
Summary: Introduces readers to Marvel character Falcon, (Sam Wilson), discusses how
he became known as Falcon, and shows how he is a great fighter and how he became
part of the Avengers team.
1. Avengers (Fictitious characters)--Juvenile fiction. 2. Superheroes--Juvenile fiction. I.
Lim, Ron, ill. II. Rosenberg, Rachelle, ill.
[E]--dc23
              2014912345

978-1-61479-359-5 (reinforced library bound edition)

Spotlight
A Division of ABDO
abdopublishing.com

Sam Wilson likes birds.
His favorite bird is the falcon.
Sam lives in New York City.

Sam tries to do what is right.
But sometimes
this gets him into trouble.

He has a pet bird.

It is a falcon named Redwing.

They fight crimes together.

Sam wants to be an Avenger.
His favorite hero is
Captain America.

One day, Sam and Redwing
get into trouble.
The crooks chase after them.

Sam and Redwing fight back.
But the crooks outnumber them!

It's a good thing Captain America
jumps in! Cap saves the day!

Sam cannot believe it!
Captain America is his idol.

Captain America sees Sam as
a good fighter.
He agrees to mentor Sam at S.H.I.E.L.D.
Sam becomes known as Falcon!

Falcon puts on wings.
He must learn to fly.

Sam tries his best.
It is not always easy.

But he wants to help people.
He wants to be a hero.

Now Sam can fly in the sky.
He can fly like a bird.

Falcon can fly up.

Falcon can swoop down.

He can perch in a tree.

Falcon can kick in midair.

Redwing goes
wherever Falcon goes.
They fly together.

Falcon can fight in the sky.

Falcon can fight on land.

Falcon is a great fighter.
Captain America
is impressed.

Captain America and Falcon are friends.
Captain America wants Falcon
to be his fighting partner.

They take on the bad guys.
They fight as a team.

Captain America battles villains on land.
Falcon charges at the villains from
the sky.

Falcon meets another S.H.I.E.L.D. agent. Her name is Black Widow. She is an Avenger, too.

Sam fights with Cap and Black Widow.
They are a great team.

Sam wants to prove he is a Super Hero.
He is ready.

Nick Fury likes Sam.

He knows Sam works hard.

He thinks Sam can help.

The Avengers want Falcon
to be part of their team!
Falcon is now an Avenger!

Falcon meets all the Avengers.
Everyone gets along.